97

School Spirit

BY JOHANNA HURWITZ

The Adventures of Ali Baba Bernstein
Aldo Applesauce
Aldo Ice Cream
Aldo Peanut Butter
Ali Baba Bernstein, Lost and Found
Baseball Fever
Busybody Nora
Class Clown
Class President
The Cold & Hot Winter
DeDe Takes Charge!
"E" Is for Elisa
The Hot & Cold Summer
Hurray for Ali Baba Bernstein
Hurricane Elaine
The Law of Gravity
Make Room for Elisa
Much Ado About Aldo
New Neighbors for Nora
New Shoes for Silvia
Nora and Mrs. Mind-Your-Own-Business
Once I Was a Plum Tree
The Rabbi's Girls
Rip-Roaring Russell
Roz and Ozzie
Russell and Elisa
Russell Rides Again
Russell Sprouts
School's Out
Superduper Teddy
Teacher's Pet
Tough-Luck Karen
The Up & Down Spring
Yellow Blue Jay

Johanna Hurwitz

School Spirit

ILLUSTRATED BY
KAREN DUGAN

Morrow Junior Books • New York

Printed in the United States of America.

1 2 3 4 5 6 7 8 9 10

Library of Congress Cataloging-in-Publication Data

Hurwitz, Johanna.
School spirit / Johanna Hurwitz; illustrated by Karen Dugan.
p.   cm.
Summary: Julio and other students at Edison-Armstrong Elementary
School organize to prevent the closing of their school.
ISBN 0-688-12825-4
[1. Schools—Fiction.]   I. Dugan, Karen, ill.   II. Title.
PZ7.H9574Sb   1994
[Fic]—dc20   93-37685   CIP   AC

In memory of my grandmother
HATTIE FRANK

Contents

1. Bad News 9

2. Locked Out 17

3. Class Discussion 30

4. The Perils of Playing Basketball 41

5. Facing the Music 52

6. The Big Cheese 63

7. Nelson's Birthday 76

8. The School-Board Meeting 88

9. Nelson Sanchez, Photographer 99

10. The Big Assembly 107

11. Repeat Performance 120

12. Front Page News 130

1

Bad News

When Julio Sanchez arrived at the Edison-Armstrong School on the first Thursday in November, he saw a group of his fifth-grade classmates talking excitedly together in the school yard. As president of Mr. Flores's class, Julio liked to be involved in everything that was going on. After all, the baseball season was over, and Julio knew that there was no way that Cricket Kaufman could be speaking about football with that sort of animation. He hurried over to hear what she was talking about.

"I don't believe it," said Franklin Dunn.

"It's terrible," groaned Cricket. "It's the worst thing that could happen."

"What is it?" asked Julio. What could have occurred overnight that was so upsetting to his classmates?

"Didn't you hear the news?" asked Cricket.

Julio shrugged his shoulders. "I didn't watch TV last night," he said.

"This wasn't on TV," said Zoe Mitchell. "But it's going to be in the newspaper today. The school board had a meeting last night. My parents were there."

"My mom was there too," added Lucas Cott.

"And they talked about closing this school next June."

"Closing the school?" said Julio. "Of course they'll do that. They always close the school when the school year is over."

"But this time they'll close it forever," said Zoe.

Julio could not believe that. "How can they do that? It's the law that we have to go to school."

"We'll still go to school, silly," said Cricket. "But it won't be in this building. And not only

that, some of us will have to go to George Washington and others will go to Thomas Jefferson." Those were the names of two other elementary schools in the district.

"It will depend on where you live," Zoe explained.

"Why would they do that?" asked Julio. None of this made sense to him.

"The school board wants to save money. So if they close this building, they can save on electricity and fuel and things like that. And they can sell our school and make a profit."

It was no wonder that Zoe seemed to know everything about it. Her father worked for the local newspaper.

"Who'd want to buy a school?" asked Arthur Lewis. It was the same question Julio had. But now that he thought about it, there had been an extraordinary number of visitors walking about their school building in recent weeks. He remembered two men poking their heads in Mr. Flores's classroom last Friday. They carried clipboards and made some notes as they stood in the doorway. And the week before, he remembered a man and a woman walking around and around the outside of the building during lunch recess. They too had been taking notes. He hadn't paid much attention to any of them at the time. Now he was willing to bet that all these visitors were part of this.

Before Zoe could go on telling any more about the proposed fate of their school, the bell rang. The fifth graders lined up and entered the building. Perhaps Mr. Flores could explain all this, Julio thought. Maybe he'd say that Zoe was wrong. It was impossible to believe that their school was going to be put up for sale.

"Calm down, calm down," Mr. Flores instructed his students when they charged into his classroom and all began speaking at once.

"But Mr. Flores. This is such bad news," said Julio. "We don't want to go to a different school. We like this one."

"That's great. I'm glad to hear that you like your school," the teacher responded. "But don't forget, you would only have another year here anyway. When you finish sixth grade in a year and a half, you'll be off to junior high. So this isn't the end of the world. It just means that you'll leave here a year earlier than you expected."

"But I wanted my brothers Marcus and

Marius to go here, just like I did," said Lucas. "Now they'll have to go to one of the other schools, and it won't be the same."

"What will happen to all the teachers?" asked Zoe. "Are you going to be fired?"

"Whatever happens to the school, they'll still need people to teach the students," said Mr. Flores. "Some of the older teachers will probably retire. Some may even retire a year or two earlier than they had originally planned. But many of the teachers will be absorbed by the other buildings."

"I want to go to the school where you are," said Julio loyally.

Mr. Flores smiled at Julio. "I don't know where I'll be or even if there will be a place for me. I'm the most junior teacher on the staff here."

Zoe gasped.

"Listen," said Mr. Flores, "before you get so upset by all this. It isn't even certain. The school board only began considering the possibility last night. There will be more discussions before a final vote is taken. Perhaps they will decide to leave this school open after all." He shrugged. "In any event, there's not much we can do about it right now. So let's get on with the business of fifth grade."

"Wait a minute," said Julio. "You mean it isn't definite? They're still talking and they could change their minds?"

"Right," said the teacher.

"Then it's up to us to make sure that they don't close the school," said Julio with determination. What kind of class president would he be if he didn't work to save his school? he said to himself.

"How can we do that?" asked Cricket. "We're just kids. We can't tell the school board what to do."

"Yes we can," insisted Julio. "Who goes to this school anyhow? Who knows the most about it? Not the school board. They're just a bunch of grown-ups. They don't come here every day. They don't know anything about us. We've got to show them what a great school this is. We've got to show that we've got school spirit."

"Yeah," said Lucas enthusiastically.

"How can we do that?" asked Cricket for the second time.

"I don't know yet," said Julio. "But I'm going to figure it out. And you're going to help me."

"I am?" asked Cricket.

"Sure. You're vice president of this class. And you've got good brains. So I'm counting on you to come up with some good ideas."

"Julio, I applaud your spirit," said Mr. Flores. "But we've got to drop this subject for the time being. It's time for arithmetic."

"All right," said Julio, sighing. He pulled out his arithmetic book and turned to the page Mr. Flores indicated. He looked at the problems on the paper in front of him. But his thoughts were elsewhere, and the problem he was thinking about was much, much harder than the one on page thirty-seven.

2

Locked Out

After their early-morning discussion, Mr. Flores refused to let the students talk about the school closing. "There is work to be done," he reminded them whenever someone tried to interrupt and ask again about the situation. "I'll schedule a time for talking about this tomorrow afternoon." Julio was determined that by the time tomorrow came, he would have some type of plan. He wasn't going to just sit by and let them sell off his school.

At noon, even though the school lunch was chicken nuggets with barbecue sauce and whipped potatoes, Julio's second-favorite school meal after pizza, he had little appetite for eating. His thoughts kept returning to the fate of the Edison-Armstrong School. How could the school board think of locking the students out of the building they had been attending for so long?

Julio was restless all day, so he was relieved when it was finally dismissal time. Unfortunately, Lucas was getting fitted for braces that day and had to rush away at once. Lucas wasn't really in a hurry to get to the orthodontist, but his mother had insisted that he not dawdle on the way home. So Julio, who usually went partway with Lucas, was on his own. He stood for a moment watching the students leaving the school. He looked at the cornerstone of the building. Its date was 1912. That was a long time ago, long before even his grandmother was born. As he walked home, Julio wondered how many students had attended classes in the school over the years. Thousands and thousands, he guessed.

When he reached his house, he stuck his hand inside his jeans pocket to feel for his key. From one pocket he pulled out two dimes and the crumpled wrapper from a piece of chewing gum. The other pocket had the note that Lucas had passed to him during social studies. CAN'T PLAY THIS AFTERNOON. ORTHODONTIST, the note said in block letters.

Julio put his hands into his jacket pockets. There was no key there either. He must have left it in the pocket of his other jeans when he threw them into the laundry hamper last night. Unlike the business of the school closing, the missing key was not a problem for Julio in the least. His grandmother, who lived with him and his two older brothers and mother, was always home.

Sure enough, Julio could hear voices talking inside. The voices were speaking in English, so Julio knew the television was on. His grandmother loved to watch the soap operas every day. Even though she could speak only in Spanish, she was able to understand the people on the programs and all of their problems. Sometimes as she watched, she would shout out advice to the characters in Spanish. Of course, the actors couldn't hear her, and even if they could, it was quite possible they didn't understand Spanish. Nevertheless, she continued to tell them what to do.

Julio rang the doorbell. He waited a full minute. When his grandmother didn't come to open the door, he rang the bell again. He pushed a long steady ring so that even though her hearing wasn't so good these days, she would not be able to miss the sound. Another minute passed, and still no one opened the door. Julio banged on the door with his fist. *"Abuela,"* he called, using the Spanish word for grandmother. "It's me, Julio." There was still no response from inside.

Julio knew his grandmother was in the apartment. She almost never went out on her own. He began to worry that she was sick. Maybe she had fainted. Maybe she was dying, he thought. She had seemed well enough when he was eating breakfast with her this morning, but one never knew with old people. Maybe she had developed some fatal illness while he was doing arithmetic problems or eating his lunch at school.

Julio tried to think of an alternate way in to his apartment. Both his brothers, Nelson and Ramon, were at work and not due home for a couple of hours. It was terrible to think that while he was standing out here, his grandmother might be lying half dead inside. The Sanchez family lived on the middle floor of a three-story building. There was an apartment below them and an apartment above. Julio seemed to remember that one of their neighbors kept a spare key for his mother in case of an emergency. This was an emergency!

Julio dropped his backpack in front of his door and raced up the stairs to the Orleanses' apartment. He rang the doorbell. After a moment, the door opened.

"Hi," Julio greeted Mrs. Orleans. "I'm locked out. Did my mother leave an extra key with you?"

"Oh, I'm sorry, Julio. I don't have one. Your mother once said that she would give me one," Mrs. Orleans explained. "But she never got around to it. Anyhow, until recently I was in and out so much that she probably thought it wouldn't be much help to you." Mrs. Orleans didn't ask Julio the whereabouts of his grandmother, which was a good thing. She was expecting a baby soon, and Julio didn't think it was a good idea to get her worried about things.

"Oh," sighed Julio with disappointment.

"Why don't you check with Mr. Findlay?" suggested Mrs. Orleans. "Since he retired, he's home most of the time. Maybe your mother gave a key to him. It would make more sense."

Julio smiled. "I bet you're right!" he said.

"If he doesn't have a key, you're welcome to come back and stay here in my apartment if you want," offered Mrs. Orleans.

"Thanks a lot," called Julio as he began running down the stairs.

On his way down to the ground floor, he gave another ring at his own bell. He didn't really expect a response, and there was none. He hurried down the next flight of stairs and rang Mr. Findlay's doorbell. There was no answer there either. It was just his luck that Mr. Findlay had picked today of all days to go off on a visit or an errand.

Julio stood thinking what his other options were in this situation. He could run to the Sycamore Shade Motel, where his mother worked as head chambermaid. But that would take too long. If his grandmother was sick, he couldn't waste time going all the way there. He thought of phoning his own apartment and asking his grandmother if she had the strength to open the door for him. The problem was that since his grandmother didn't speak English, she never answered the telephone.

Julio went back up to his own door and rang the bell once again. As before, nothing happened.

On the landing where Julio was standing there was a window adjacent to the living-room window in his apartment. He had never tried it, but Julio was pretty sure that if he climbed out of that window on the landing, he would be able to climb into his living room.

He went over to the window and released the catch. The window frame had been painted during the summer, so it didn't slide open as easily as it had in the past. But Julio figured he didn't have to open it all the way. Halfway would be enough for him to get out.

When the window was open, Julio crawled out and stood with his feet on the window ledge and his back to the street. He was lucky that the ledge was wide enough for his whole foot. His fingers grasped the edge of the window frame. He saw that the distance between the window where he was standing and his family's living room was only a few feet. He was pleased to see that his living-room window was open a couple of inches at the bottom. That would make it easier for him to open it wider.

Julio knew better than to look down. Once, a couple of years ago, he had sat on the roof of his friend Lucas's house. It had been fun until he looked down. So now he avoided the chance of making himself dizzy by keeping his eyes on the window.

Cautiously Julio inched his feet along the window ledge. When he reached the end, he took a deep breath and stretched out his right foot until it was resting on the ledge of his living-room window. This was a piece of cake, he thought, grinning to himself. He didn't need a key at all. He wished all problems could be solved so easily. Too bad there wasn't an equally simple way to keep his school from being shut down.

He peeked through the living-room window and saw his grandmother slumped over on the sofa facing the window. Julio felt sick at the sight. His grandmother had either fainted or died. He could hardly bear to look at her. He could hear the voices on the television continuing with their drama even without an audience.

Julio blinked back some tears. It was good that he was here. He hadn't ever studied CPR, but he had seen it done in the movies. He might have to get his grandmother breathing again.

Holding tightly to the window frame, Julio

used his right foot to slide the window up higher. Suddenly he heard a loud scream. The sound startled Julio so much that he almost lost his hold on the window. Luckily his right foot was already inside the living room. As he ducked under the raised sash, Julio heard another scream. It was even louder than the first.

Inside the apartment, Julio discovered that his grandmother was now sitting up with her eyes open. He realized that the screams he heard had come from her.

"Julio!" she shouted.

"*Abuela!*" Julio responded. He jumped down from the window and ran to give her a hug. How wonderful that she was conscious again, he thought, though it was too bad that he couldn't try CPR. He bet he could have saved her if it was necessary.

"What's wrong?" he asked his grandmother. "Why are you screaming? Do you have a bad pain? Should I call an ambulance?" he asked anxiously.

Julio's grandmother began jabbering away rapidly in Spanish. Even though he couldn't speak Spanish, Julio usually understood what she was saying. This afternoon, the words poured out of her mouth so fast that he couldn't make out anything.

"Is it your head?" he asked. "Or your heart? What hurts?"

"My eyes!" Julio's grandmother screamed in Spanish. "They have never seen such a terrible sight. You could have killed yourself. Why did you come through the window? Suppose you had fallen. Why didn't you use the door like you do every other day?"

"I didn't have my key," Julio explained. "I rang the bell, but you didn't answer. I was afraid you were dying. And when I looked through the window, you were keeled over. I thought you were dead."

"Dead? I was sleeping," shouted Julio's grandmother. "But I could have had a heart attack at the sight of you coming in the window."

As a result of the real-life drama in the Sanchez living room, there was a lot to talk about at suppertime.

"You must never climb through the window again," said Mrs. Sanchez sternly when she had heard the whole story. "Suppose you had fallen."

"But I didn't fall," said Julio.

"If you ever get locked out again, you have two choices. Walk over to the Sycamore Shade Motel or just wait here till one of your brothers comes home. Do you understand?"

"I didn't want to waste any time," Julio explained. "I thought Grandma was dying. How was I to know she was taking a nap?"

"You should have listened for the snores," laughed Ramon, the older of Julio's brothers.

"Such a lot of excitement just because an old lady wants to get a little sleep," Julio's grandmother complained.

"Well, it's all over now. And everything is fine." Mrs. Sanchez smiled. Her tone was no longer angry. "No one is ill. Usually Julio has good common sense, and I'm sure I can count on him not to frighten you again," she said, turning to her mother.

"I guess I was thinking about other things," Julio admitted. "I have a lot on my mind today." He was embarrassed at the way the afternoon had turned out.

"What's bothering you?" asked Mrs. Sanchez, looking concerned.

Julio recounted to his family the bad news about the Edison-Armstrong School.

"Forget about it," said Nelson. "There's nothing you can do."

Ramon and Mrs. Sanchez agreed. "Next year you'll go to another school," said Ramon. "It's not the end of the world."

"You don't understand," said Julio. "There's a lot of memories and history at Edison-Armstrong. I don't want to see it all disappear."

"Good luck," said Ramon. "But I don't think you'll be able to change anything. If the school board wants to close down the building, you can't stop them."

"I'm going to try," said Julio. "I don't want to be locked out of my school next year."

3

Class Discussion

On Fridays, Mr. Flores brought his guitar to school. The last hour of the day was devoted to singing and talk. It was a relaxed and friendly way to end the week, and Julio and all his classmates looked forward to it. In fact, they were almost sorry when the dismissal bell rang and school was over for the week.

This Friday, however, it didn't look as if Mr. Flores would do any guitar playing. The last hour was going to be devoted to a discussion of the fate of their school. It was nothing to sing about. There had been a lengthy article in the newspaper yesterday explaining the decision before the school board. Cricket Kaufman had cut it out and brought it into class. During the lunch hour, Julio had hardly been aware that he was eating his favorite school lunch: pizza squares with pepperoni, tossed salad, fruit cocktail, and chocolate milk. He carefully studied every word of the article. It gave all the details of why the district was considering the proposed closing, and it explained how much money could be saved.

Now Mr. Flores handed out a flyer on yellow paper to each of the students. It had been prepared by the school for the students to take home to their parents. Much of the information from the newspaper article was repeated on the sheet. It also listed the day and date a month off when the school board would next be meeting to discuss the proposed school closing.

Lucas began to fold his copy of the flyer into a paper airplane. A couple of the other boys noticed and did the same thing. Julio was tempted too. A sheet of paper like this was just begging to be transformed into an airplane. But Julio resisted the urge. He was the class president, and his class was discussing something very serious.

"I don't see why it's our school that has to be closed," Cricket protested. "If they want to close a school, why don't they close one of the other ones?"

"Yeah," agreed several of the other students.

"Well, aside from the fact that this is the building where you go to school, what makes this place so special?" asked Mr. Flores. "Aren't all schools the same?"

"Oh, no," protested Zoe. She was the expert

on this subject. "This school is friendlier. There's a nice feeling here. Even though I'm still new in the community, I think it's great that Cricket's mother went to this school."

"My father went here too," said Sara Jane Cushman.

"So did mine," said Arthur Lewis. "Maybe they were in the same class."

"You like the continuity then," said Mr. Flores. He wrote the word CONTINUITY on the chalkboard.

As the teacher turned his back, one of the yellow paper airplanes flew across the room. It was followed by a second one. Mr. Flores turned around and faced the class while the second one was still airborne.

"Now hear this," announced Mr. Flores. "Due to conditions beyond your control the airport is closed and all planes are grounded." He walked over and picked up the two yellow paper planes from the floor. He unfolded them and flattened the sheets out. "This is important information for your parents. If you are missing your notice, I recommend that you come and take one from my desk before you go home."

Julio turned and grinned at Lucas. Mr. Flores was allowing his friend to reclaim his yellow sheet anonymously. No wonder Julio liked their teacher so much.

"I think it's great that this school is old. It's been around here for a long time," said Zoe. "It has a nice old-school smell and feel about it. Not like my last school, which was bright and shiny new and felt more like a hospital than a school."

SENSE OF HISTORY, Mr. Flores wrote on the board.

This time there were no airplanes flying when his back was turned.

"How old is this building anyhow?" asked Arthur.

"It's more than eighty years old," said Cricket before Julio could respond. "It says so in the article."

"Wow. That's how old my great-grandfather is," said Sara Jane.

"Maybe Edison went here," suggested Julio. "Maybe that's the way it got his name."

"You could look that up," said the teacher. "And while you're at it, why don't you find out who Armstrong is too."

"I know. I know who that is," shouted Cricket.

Julio looked at Cricket's face. It was red with excitement. She just loved knowing an answer that no one else knew.

"Armstrong is Henrietta Armstrong, who was the first principal of this school. She worked here for forty years. Her picture is in the lobby."

"Oh, right," agreed Julio. He must have passed that picture of the white-haired old lady a hundred thousand times. He saw it and he didn't see it. Now he'd have to make sure to take a good look at it on his way out of the building today. Imagine coming to this building every school day for forty years.

"It doesn't seem nice to honor someone by naming a building after them and then selling the building or tearing it down," said Arthur.

"I sure wouldn't like it if someone did that to me," said Cricket.

"Don't worry, no one is ever going to name a building after you," said Lucas.

"Yes they will," Cricket insisted. "You just wait until I'm the first woman president of the United States. They'll probably want to call this school the Edison-Armstrong-Kaufman School."

"That's too much for anyone to say, and besides, they won't be able to do it if this school is closed," Lucas pointed out.

"I have a suggestion," said Mr. Flores, interrupting Cricket and Lucas. "Who would like to be on a committee to find out what was happening in the world eighty years ago? We can make a time line. Eighty years ago in this community, in the United States, and in the world."

"Ooh, me, me," said Cricket, raising her hand.

It was just the type of project she liked.

"Me too," said Zoe.

"Great," said Mr. Flores.

Julio raised his hand.

Mr. Flores nodded in recognition. "Yes, Julio. Do you want to be on the committee too?"

"I want us to do something to rally all the students and to make a difference. Can't we get the school board to change their minds? How about writing them a letter about how we feel. Maybe all the other classes would write letters too. We should make posters to decorate the halls. Make up a school cheer and a school song. Maybe if we can show the school board that we all have a lot of school spirit, they'll change their minds about sending all of us off to other schools."

Anne Crosby raised her hand. "I want to write a song," she said.

Everyone was surprised by this offer. "Are you a relative of Bing Crosby?" asked Cricket. "I saw him singing in an old movie on TV."

Anne blushed. "No," she said. "But I'd like to make up a song anyway. I like to write poems."

"Great," said Mr. Flores. "If you write a song,

I'll accompany you on my guitar." Mr. Flores looked around the room. "Any other ideas?" he asked.

"Maybe we could design T-shirts for everyone in the school," suggested Zoe. "If we all walked around in matching shirts, it would show that we all belong together."

"Blue ones," suggested Cricket.

"No, black," someone else called out.

"It could be like an art project," said Julio. "Maybe the art teacher could help us. If we made a design and everyone brought a plain white shirt to school, we could all make our own shirts in art."

Mr. Flores nodded his head as he wrote TOGETHERNESS on the board.

"I have an idea," offered Sara Jane. "Maybe some of our parents who attended this school would come and tell what it was like in the olden times."

Mr. Flores began a second column of ideas. He wrote LETTER, GUESTS, T-SHIRTS, SONG.

"I think we should plant flowers all around the school yard and do other things to make the school more beautiful," suggested a girl named Joyce Howe. "If we make it look prettier, they will forget that the building is so old. In the newspaper article it said that this school is very shabby."

"It's the wrong season for planting flowers. They'd all die in the cold. But we should be better about picking up trash," suggested Zoe. "I noticed a lot of papers flying around in the yard during lunch recess. It doesn't look very nice."

"I saw a couple of soda cans too," said Arthur.

"That's not our garbage," Lucas complained. "People waiting at the bus stop on the corner by the school are the ones who throw a lot of that stuff in the yard."

"We still should clean it up," said Zoe. "If someone from the school board comes by, they don't know whose junk it is. They just see it's in our school yard. It looks like we don't care."

"Sometimes there's garbage inside the school too," said Julio, feeling guilty. Just this morning he had kicked a crumpled ball of paper from one end of the hallway to the other without picking it up.

Mr. Flores added the word CLEAN-UP to his second list. Before he could write anything more, however, the dismissal bell rang.

"Already?" complained Julio. It seemed too soon for the school day to end.

Mr. Flores turned to face the students. "All these ideas are called brainstorming," he said. "Every time one of you made a suggestion, it gave another one of you an idea. You start working on your ideas, and a week from now we'll pick up at this point. If you want, over the weekend you can write a letter to the school board. Next week we can incorporate everyone's ideas and write a class letter for students to sign."

"All right," said Julio. He felt full of energy and excitement from the class discussion. He couldn't wait to speak with some of the other class presidents and the students in the other rooms. In one of the sixth grades there was a tall and very popular girl named Jennifer Harper who was class president. She always had a group of her classmates around her, and they hung on every word she said. Julio had a feeling she would be a good ally for this cause. He'd have to make a point of speaking to her as soon as possible. For the first time in his life Julio regretted that it was Friday afternoon. Now he'd have to wait until school opened again on Monday morning. What a pain!

4

The Perils of Playing Basketball

Julio did other things over the weekend besides think about the Edison-Armstrong School. He shot baskets with his brother Nelson in the high-school yard on Saturday morning. Then, when Nelson went off to his job at the supermarket, Julio vacuumed their whole apartment for his mother. He knew his mother counted on his help, but he'd be glad when he was old enough to get a real, paying job like both his brothers. It rained on Sunday, so in the afternoon Julio went with Ramon and Nelson to a really exciting movie. He loved it when the three of them went places together.

Yet in between his weekend activities, Julio found time to write a letter to the school board and cook up schemes to raise the school spirit of the kids at Edison-Armstrong. Jogging to school on Monday morning, he started thinking of all those slogans he'd picked up over the years in social studies or while watching game shows on TV. They suddenly took on a new meaning now that he had a cause too.

I have not yet begun to fight. Was it John Paul Jones who had said that, or someone else? Julio couldn't remember. But it was a great line. Julio liked it. He repeated it to himself a couple of times.

Fifty-four forty or fight, he suddenly recalled. It was another of those old historic slogans. It sounded more like a football score than a slogan, but he remembered learning that those words had once rallied the country.

Remember the Alamo—they could change that to *Remember the Edison-Armstrong.*

I cannot tell a lie. I chopped down the cherry tree. That's what George Washington told his parents when he was a little kid and got into mischief. It was probably the first quotation that Julio had learned when he started school. It was one he'd never forget, but it didn't apply in this situation.

Then he remembered, *I know not what course others will take; but as for me give me Edison-Armstrong, or give me death!* Patrick Henry had wanted liberty. Julio didn't really want to die over the business of closing the school, but it sure sounded serious.

Outside the school, he stopped to talk with Matthew Lang, who was president of his sixth-grade class. Jennifer Harper was walking by, and without Julio even calling to her, she came over and joined their conversation.

"We're graduating, so it doesn't really affect us," said Matthew, shrugging when Julio explained why he wanted to keep the school from closing.

"It does affect us," said Jennifer. "I see what Julio means. How can we take our own kids to see the school we went to if it isn't here for them to see?"

"What kids?" asked Matthew. "I'm not going to get married. I don't have to worry about any old kids."

"How do you know now that you won't change your mind?" asked Julio. "And besides, even if you don't have kids, that's no reason to close down this school."

"Don't worry. I'll organize everyone," Jennifer promised Julio. "We'll show the school board that we kids care about our school even if they don't."

The bell rang, and Jennifer ran off to join her classmates. Julio stood for a moment watching as Matthew walked off too. He had hoped Jennifer would want to get involved. He knew he needed her and other people to help him. But he was surprised by the enthusiastic way she was ready to take over his project. He didn't want that. He'd have to keep an eye on her.

I have not yet begun to fight, he said to himself again as he entered the school building.

At ten o'clock on Monday mornings, Mr. Flores's section of fifth grade always had phys. ed. Julio knew that his teacher thought it was bad timing. He wanted to use the students' early-morning energy for things like arithmetic and language arts. But Julio loved phys. ed. and would have been pleased to be scheduled to do activities in the gym from nine A.M. straight through the day. This morning when he lined up with his classmates, he was eager to show off his new skill with the hook shot. Nelson had drilled him, and now he rarely missed.

Lucas and Julio were at the end of the line. Julio held back a little till there was a small distance between him and his classmates. Then he pretended that he was dribbling a basketball down the hallway.

"Throw it here," called Lucas. His new braces gleamed in his mouth as he spoke. Julio took the imaginary ball and threw it with his right hand.

Lucas caught the ball and ran in a little circle, dribbling it too. Then he threw it to Julio.

Julio couldn't wait to get to the gym. Grabbing the imaginary ball, he leaped into the air, and using the fire-alarm box in the hallway in place of a basketball hoop, he aimed his shot. His hand slapped the corner of the alarm box, and suddenly the loud clanging of the fire gong began.

The noise startled both boys. It took Julio a second to realize that he was the cause of all the racket. "Oh, wow," he groaned to himself. How could such a little tap on the alarm box have done that? He looked over at Lucas. His friend seemed stunned at the unexpected turn in their ball game.

"It must be the end of the quarter," said Julio, trying to make a joke of it. He just couldn't believe that he had done such a thing.

The rest of the fifth grade had made an about-face. "Hurry up, you guys," called Cricket in that bossy way she sometimes used. "This is a fire drill. We have to evacuate the building at once."

"Oh, right," said Julio.

He grabbed Lucas by the arm and began walking toward the nearest exit with the rest of his class. None of them seemed to realize that he was responsible for turning on the alarm.

The class went outside the building and stood on the sidewalk near the school with the rest of the student body. Everyone was jumping up and down in place and hugging themselves. It was too cold to be outside without a jacket unless there was an honest-to-goodness emergency. Most times when there was a fire drill there was either warm weather or enough time to grab warm clothing. All the teachers were talking together.

"Did you get a memo about this drill?" one asked another.

"There was nothing in my box," said another.

"My class was in the middle of a test. Now I'll have to call it off and make up a new one."

Imagine that, thought Julio. His mother always said you learn something new every day. "I never knew that teachers were warned in advance about fire drills," he said to Lucas, who was standing beside him. "I thought they were just as surprised by them as we are. And all these years I've been praying for a fire drill to interrupt an arithmetic test. It was all a waste. Teachers wouldn't schedule a test if they knew there was going to be a drill."

Then something happened that had never happened during a fire drill in all Julio's years of school. In the distance he heard a siren, which got louder and louder as the fire engines got closer to the school building. He looked over at Lucas. Did Lucas realize that the school alarm system was hooked up to the local fire department? Hooked up. He had used his hook shot, and look what a mess he had created.

As if in answer to his friend's thoughts, Lucas looked over at Julio. "If they plan the fire drills in advance," he whispered, "they can notify the fire department and the trucks won't come. This time no one told them not to come."

Lucas looked frightened. It was the way Julio felt. They were in a heap of trouble now. That was certain.

The engines pulled up in front of the Edison-Armstrong School. No sooner did the trucks come to a halt than fire fighters were jumping off and pulling out the long black hoses that were attached to the truck. Four men rushed into the front entrance of the building. Julio guessed they didn't want to waste a moment in case there was a fire burning inside.

Two little girls in Mrs. Greenberg's first-grade class, which was standing nearby, began to cry. "Our school is on fire," cried one girl, who had long blond braids.

"And my doll is inside. I brought her for show-and-tell," cried the other.

"My new jacket is inside too," called out a first-grade boy.

Mrs. Greenberg had her hands full calming her anxious students. Julio looked at Lucas for support. He wished someone would calm him.

What did they do to people who called in false alarms to the fire department? Did they go to jail? Even as that thought was going through Julio's mind, a police car pulled up behind the fire trucks.

Mr. Herbertson, the school's principal, walked out of the front door of the school building, accompanied by the firemen and three other people Julio had never seen before. They weren't teachers at the school, and the way they were dressed, they didn't look like parents who had come for conferences about their kids. All of them stood at the top of the steps, talking together. Then Mr. Herbertson waved to all the teachers and students. "It was a false alarm," he called. "The all-clear bell is going to ring in another minute."

There had been a time when Julio had been scared of Mr. Herbertson and his big dark eyes, which all the kids called spooky. However, recently he had gotten to speak with the principal a couple of times, and he had decided that he was a really nice person. He was sure Mr. Herbertson wouldn't say the same thing about Julio if he knew that he was the one responsible for the false alarm.

A moment later loud clangs sounded. They

were the usual signal to return to class after a fire drill.

"Thank goodness," said Cricket. "I'm so cold, my teeth are chattering. We'll probably all come down with pneumonia now too."

"Thank goodness it wasn't a real fire," added Zoe.

"I wonder who called in the false alarm?" said Arthur.

"Who would do an awful thing like that?" Cricket asked.

"Yeah," said Julio, pretending not to know the answer to this mystery. He also wondered just what his chances were of getting sick. A good case of pneumonia might be preferable to allowing anyone to discover that he was the one who had triggered the alarm system.

5

Facing the Music

Lunch that Monday was cheeseburgers, coleslaw, potato chips, and canned peaches. It wasn't Julio's favorite of the hot meals offered by the school, but he wasn't known to ever leave any of it either.

"Are you sick or something?" Arthur asked Julio. He pointed to the tray where Julio's cheeseburger sat with only two bites missing. Julio hadn't even eaten any of his chips.

"He's probably coming down with pneumonia," said Cricket. She was eagerly waiting to see who would be the first of their class to collapse with this ailment.

"I feel fine," Julio protested. "I'm just not hungry."

How could he feel hungry? Shortly before lunchtime, Mr. Herbertson's voice had come over the school public-address system.

"It is the belief of the school-board members who have been visiting our school this morning that the false alarm we had was caused by old and faulty wiring. The electric company is sending an inspector to check this out. However, if it is discovered that a student was responsible for sounding the alarm, it will be very serious business. I hope that we are correct in blaming the wiring. Fire drills are for your safety and protection. I want every student in this school to know and understand the Aesop fable of the boy who cried wolf. It is an old tale, but it is as relevant today as it was when it was first recorded in ancient Greece."

Of course, after that announcement, activities stopped in Mr. Flores's classroom and in all the other rooms in the school. Every teacher retold the well-known fable. Julio, who had never in his life seen a live wolf, squirmed in his seat. Lucas had once seen a wolf at the zoo. He looked just as uncomfortable as Julio during the class discussion about the fable. After all, he had witnessed his friend causing the false alarm. In fact, if he hadn't thrown the imaginary ball back to him, perhaps Julio would never have jumped high enough to hit the alarm box. The two boys eyed one another warily. Neither one knew how they would get out of this situation.

So now in the lunchroom, Julio just looked at his cheeseburger without any appetite.

"Knock, knock," said Arthur. He poked Julio to get his attention. "Knock, knock," he said again.

"Who's there?" asked Julio, pretending to be interested.

"Goat."

"Goat who?"

"Goat-tell the principal this food stinks." Arthur grinned. He looked pleased with himself and his punch line. But for Julio, this was no time for making jokes.

Lucas had brought his lunch from home. He removed the baloney sandwich and the apple from their paper bag and did something he hadn't done in a long, long time. In his nervousness, he unconsciously blew up the brown paper bag, and when it was filled with air, he popped it.

A startled fourth-grade girl at the next table let out a shriek of surprise and knocked over her container of milk at the same time. And someone else stood up and pretended that he had been shot. None of it was very bad mischief. However, it all happened just as the three school-board members, together with Mr. Herberston, walked into the lunch room. Instantly everyone in the lunch room froze. The only motion in the room was the slow drip, drip, drip as the spilled milk left the next table and landed on the floor. It was like a magic spell had been placed on the students.

Darn them, thought Julio, hardly daring to breathe. Why don't those board members go home and leave us alone?

Lucas and Julio watched anxiously as Mr. Herbertson and the three visitors walked across the room. Julio looked down at his tray of food. He wondered if his face gave away his guilt. From the corner of his eye, he saw Mr. Herbertson bend down and pick up a straw wrapper from the floor. The principal didn't seem to notice Julio at all. Julio let out his breath as he watched Mr. Herbertson give a handful of paper napkins to a fourth-grade boy.

"Clean up that mess," he said, pointing to the puddle of milk on the floor.

When Mr. Herbertson and the board members left the room, the students' voices immediately began again. "Listen," said Julio, leaning over and speaking softly so only Lucas would hear him. "I'm going to tell him I did it. It will only be worse if he finds out on his own."

"How can he find out?" asked Lucas nervously.

"I don't know. Maybe they'll find my fingerprints on the alarm box."

"Yikes," said Lucas. "I never thought of that."

When the twenty minutes allocated to eating was over, the students grabbed their jackets and went out into the yard. As they approached the door, Julio saw the three school-board members leaving the building. Impulsively he decided to go to Mr. Herbertson and give his confession right now. He wanted to get the terrible moment over with as soon as possible.

"I'm coming with you," said Lucas, sticking close to Julio.

"Are you nuts?" asked Julio. "We don't both have to get into trouble. You didn't do anything."

"I threw the ball to you," said Lucas.

"I don't know if Herbertson is going to buy that. We don't even have a ball to show him," sighed Julio as they reached the principal's office.

The school secretary was not at her desk. The boys could see Mr. Herbertson sitting inside the inner office, however. Julio walked forward and knocked hesitantly on the open door. Mr. Herbertson looked up.

"Julio?" he asked. "What can I do for you?"

Julio reminded himself of the father of his country. He took a deep breath, and then he said, "Mr. Herbertson, I cannot tell a lie." Once he began, the rest of the famous phrase just burst out of his mouth as well. "I chopped down the cherry tree."

The puzzled expression left the principal's face. He smiled at the boys. "This school has a variety of problems facing it at the moment and a dozen or so maple trees all around it," he said, laughing. "But one thing we don't have is a cherry tree."

Julio felt his face grow hot. "I meant, I cannot tell a lie," he said. "The other words were a mistake. But I want to tell you the truth like George

Washington and Honest Abe Lincoln."

"What about?" asked the principal.

"I caused the false alarm."

Mr. Herbertson jumped up from his seat. "Julio. I can't believe it. You're not the type of kid to do something so irresponsible."

"Yes I am," said Julio, his head drooping with shame and embarrassment. "I really did it. I'm guilty. But I'm guilty with an explanation. I swear I didn't do it on purpose. I accidentally hit the alarm box."

"That's right," said Lucas, who had been standing off to the side. "We were playing basketball and we were dribbling the ball back and forth as we went down the hallway."

Julio looked anxiously at Mr. Herbertson. He wondered if Lucas's words helped his case or made it worse. The boys weren't supposed to play basketball, real or imaginary, as they walked down the halls.

"Let me get this straight," said the principal, his voice rising with anger. "You were playing basketball and your ball hit the alarm box. Since when do you play ball in the hallway?"

"We didn't have a ball," Julio explained. "We

just pretended we did." Julio began to demonstrate by bouncing an imaginary ball in the principal's office. It was probably the only time in the history of Edison-Armstrong School that a ball had been bounced in that room—even if it was only an invisible one.

Eventually Mr. Herbertson got the picture.

"So you see, I came to confess," said Julio. "But I want you to know I didn't do it on purpose."

Mr. Herbertson stood shaking his head. "It was my plan, if it was discovered that the false alarm had been set by a student, to see that he or she was suspended for a week. But I understand that you didn't mean to do it."

Julio and Lucas looked at each other. Suspension was just about the worst punishment you could get.

"It was an accident," said Lucas softly.

"Since it wasn't intentional on your part, I won't suspend you," said Mr. Herbertson.

Both boys gave sighs of relief. Julio smiled at the principal. "Thanks," he said.

"Instead, I want you each to write me a letter describing the proper conduct when walking through the halls of a school building. I want it on my desk first thing tomorrow morning. Do you understand?"

"Yes," said Julio. He was no longer smiling. It seemed all he did these days was write letters.

"Yes," said Lucas.

"All right," said the principal. "At least I don't have to worry about faulty wiring around here. There are enough other problems." He gave a sigh.

"That's something I want to talk to you about too," said Julio. "I don't think we should let them close this school. I think we've got to fight to keep it open."

"I'm glad you like the school so much," said Mr. Herbertson. "It's a compliment to your teachers. But my hands are tied. I just have to wait and go with the board's decision. Of course, they haven't voted yet. But in my opinion, it doesn't look good for the future of this building."

"My hands aren't tied," said Julio, stretching out his fingers. "And neither are Lucas's. He's going to help me. I want to organize all the kids. We're not the only ones who feel this way. I've begun talking to the others. Jennifer Harper, who's president of her sixth-grade class, is going to help. And there will be others."

Mr. Herbertson's dark eyes beamed at Julio. "I can't begin to tell you how good I feel that you care so much," he said. "I won't stop you. Go to it."

"I'm going right now," said Julio, jumping up from his seat and pulling Lucas along too.

"Just one thing to remember," said the principal.

"What?" asked the boys.

"Sound the alarm for the school, but don't ring any false alarms."

6

The Big Cheese

With the principal's approval behind him, Julio was ready to start on his campaign to save the school. So was Jennifer Harper.

Almost as soon as he arrived at school the next day, Julio overheard one student telling another that Jennifer Harper had big plans to save Edison-Armstrong. The next thing he knew, Jennifer ran up to him in the school yard to invite him to a meeting at her home that very afternoon.

Amazingly, eleven fifth- and sixth-grade students showed up at Jennifer's home after school. Most of them had skipped after-school dance class or piano lessons to be able to come. It meant that all of them felt this was very important. But first there was the business of sodas.

"Who wants a Coke?" Jennifer asked. She was sitting on the floor of the wood-paneled den, and the coffee table in front of her was covered with cans of soda. There was every flavor you could think of. Julio reached for root beer. There were big bowls of potato chips and pretzels and popcorn too. Julio appreciated the hospitality, but he hoped this gathering wasn't going to turn into nothing more than a party. He was relieved when Jennifer turned off the CD player. They didn't need background music at this meeting. This was serious business.

Jennifer's house was fancier than any of the homes of Julio's friends. He guessed that if his own home had a big room like this, he'd give parties all the time himself.

"Don't hog all the chips," Matthew Lang complained when Jason Frankel took a huge handful.

Jason was a class president too. In fact, eight of the eleven kids sitting around eating and drinking were presidents of their classes. Only Julio had brought along some assistants. Cricket was class vice president, and Zoe was Cricket's best friend. Lucas was Julio's best friend, so they all had to be in this together.

"All right," said Jennifer, banging her soda can on the table to get the group's attention. "We need a name."

"Name?" asked Julio. He didn't know what Jennifer meant.

"Sure. If we are a committee to work to save our school, we need to have a name. Something with initials that form a word. I was thinking about KOSO."

"What's that?" asked Zoe.

"Keep Our School Open," said Jennifer with pride.

"KOSO sounds kind of stupid to me," said Julio.

"KOSO," giggled Lucas. "Kind Of Stupid Organization."

"Well, do you have a better name?" asked Jennifer, daring him to come up with an alternative.

"Just a minute," said Cricket. She had come to the meeting equipped with a notebook and pencil. Now she began scribbling furiously and mumbling to herself. "How about EASE? Edison-Armstrong Student Energy?"

"I don't think that's better than KOSO," Jennifer said.

"I think it's silly to waste time arguing about a name for ourselves," Julio complained. "We want to save our school, not form student groups with clever names."

"That's it," said Cricket. "S.O.S. Save Our School. It's simple, it's catchy, and S.O.S. already has a meaning that alerts everyone to action."

"Good," said Julio. "I like it." He smiled appreciatively at Cricket. Sometimes she could be a pain, but she could also come through at important moments.

"Yeah. S.O.S. That's good," agreed Matthew.

"I like it too," said Jason.

Everyone seemed to like the new name except Jennifer. But she knew when she was beaten. "All right," she agreed reluctantly.

So finally the students were ready to get down to the real substance of their meeting. "The school board is going to debate the business of closing our school in three weeks," said Jennifer. "So that's all the time we have to make people aware of how we feel."

"It's not just how we feel," Zoe pointed out. "It's why they shouldn't take such a drastic step."

"Our class is writing a letter to the school board," said Julio. "I think all the classes should write letters."

"We need to do more than just write a letter," said Jennifer. "We have to advertise how we feel." She banged her soda can on the table for emphasis. "I think we should make posters, T-shirts, bumper stickers. We've got to mobilize everyone and plaster this whole town with the message that they should not close Edison-Armstrong."

"We can use the S.O.S. slogan," began Julio, eager to contribute something that the group would agree to. Jennifer cut him off.

"No," said Jennifer. "I've figured out something better. First off, T-shirts."

"Red," said Matthew Lang. "Let's make them red."

Julio looked at Matthew. He had blond hair and he looked good in red. He had come in wearing a red jacket, and now that he had taken it off you could see his red-and-white-checked shirt.

"Blue," said Julio to spite Matthew. "I think they should be blue. And they should say *I love Edison-Armstrong School.*"

"Boring," said Jennifer. "We need something with more zip. Bright red shirts. On the front they'll say *Keep the lights on at Edison-Armstrong School,* and on the back there should be a picture of a light bulb. Edison, light bulb, get it?" she asked the group.

"Hey, that's neat," said Jason Frankel. "I like it."

"Me too. Me too," the other sixth graders agreed.

"I checked it out with Mrs. Boomsma, the art teacher," said Jennifer. "She said that if everyone brought in a plain white T-shirt from home, we could make the shirts as an art project. So it won't cost any money at all."

Julio looked at Jennifer. The idea of going to the art teacher was the same thing he had thought of. But he hadn't had a chance to talk to Mrs. Boomsma about it yet. Somehow Jennifer had. She was like a steamroller. In the little more than twenty-four hours since he suggested to her that they should do something, she had come up with all these ideas, talked with teachers, planned this meeting, and even bought refreshments. He used to believe that Cricket would be the first woman president of the United States. At this rate, Cricket would have to wait in line and take office after Jennifer Harper retired.

"Yellow," Julio called out.

"What?" asked Jennifer.

"The shirts should be yellow, not red. Like light," he explained.

"That's great," said Zoe. "I love that idea."

"Make up your mind," Jennifer grumbled. "First you said blue. Now you say yellow."

"Yellow," said Julio. He felt his face turning red. He hadn't realized that Jennifer could be so bossy and unpleasant.

"Yellow is the best color with those words," said Zoe.

"Okay," agreed Jennifer after a moment. "We'll dye the shirts yellow."

Julio smiled at Zoe. Finally he had made a point.

"Okay, next on the list," Jennifer said, consulting a notebook. "Next is publicity. We have to

make the whole community aware about what is happening."

"My father works for the newspaper. He said if we wanted to write something, he'd see that it got published," offered Zoe.

"Great. I'll take care of that," said Jennifer.

Julio looked at his classmates. Cricket's mouth was hanging open. He knew that she and Zoe had been planning to write something for the newspaper.

"I thought we'd print up some bumper stickers," said Jennifer.

"They could say *Honk if you like Edison-Armstrong*," suggested Julio.

"If we do bumper stickers, we need a better message," said Jennifer. "It will get too noisy in town with that one. I'll think of something else to say."

Some of the other kids began to make suggestions.

"*Edison-Armstrong: Worth the drive.*"

"*I'd drive a mile to Edison-Armstrong.*"

"*All aboard for Edison-Armstrong.*" That last suggestion was from Cricket.

"That sounds like a bumper sticker for a train," said Jennifer.

"I think it's the best bumper slogan we've come up with," said Julio, loyally defending Cricket's words. "My brother collects bumper stickers. They say all kinds of things."

"Yeah. His brother Nelson has a thousand stickers," Lucas agreed.

"How many cars does he have?" asked Matthew.

"None. He's too young to get a driver's license. But you can collect bumper stickers at any age," said Julio. He didn't add that even if Nelson had a driver's license, he wouldn't have the money to buy himself a car.

"Okay," Jennifer agreed. "The bumper sticker will say *All aboard for Edison-Armstrong.*"

Julio sighed. His team had won another point. Working with Jennifer was really tough.

Jennifer's mother came into the room to see how the meeting was going. "I just want to tell you that I've been on the phone with the executive board of the Parent-Teacher Organization," she told the children. "We are going to do all we can to keep Edison-Armstrong open. None of us with younger children want them riding a bus to a school on the other side of town."

Julio looked around. He didn't know if Jennifer had a younger brother or sister. He also had the feeling that Mrs. Harper had missed the point. He would have loved riding a school bus and in fact had always felt a little bit cheated that he lived within walking distance of Edison-Armstrong. The point was the school had a history and a tradition that shouldn't be destroyed.

"We're going to pack the board meeting," Mrs. Harper assured the S.O.S. committee. "They'll see that they can't make these big decisions behind our back." Mrs. Harper picked up a couple of empty soda cans and left the room.

"I'm glad your mother is on our side," said Matthew. "She sounds very determined."

"She is," said Jennifer. "And so am I."

"Cricket and I are doing research about what was happening in the world eighty years ago, when our school was built," said Zoe.

"And one of the girls in our class said she's going to write a song," Lucas remembered.

"I've decided we should plan a large assembly program," said Jennifer. "Then we can present your information about the past and sing the song and make it into a real rally for Edison-Armstrong."

"That was my plan," said Julio, but no one was listening to him. Everyone was talking at once about all their ideas. By the time all the soda and the popcorn, potato chips, and pretzels were consumed, everyone was bursting with ideas as well as with snack food.

"That was a great meeting," said Cricket as she walked out into the street with her classmates. "I never knew anyone with so many super ideas as Jennifer Harper."

"The idea for the T-shirt is really neat," said Zoe.

"We can all wear them when we have the assembly program," said Lucas.

Julio listened to his friends rediscussing the things that they had been talking about all afternoon. None of them seemed to mind that Jennifer Harper had taken over. Just because they were meeting in her house and just because she was in sixth grade, she seemed to think she was in charge of everything, he fumed to himself. She thought she was big stuff, busy bossing everyone around. It was a wonder that anyone had a chance to say any-thing when she was around. In fact, he had con-tributed almost nothing.

"See you tomorrow," he called to his friends as he took the turn toward his home.

Jennifer Harper might be a big cheese, he thought to himself. But the worse thing was that after sitting in her house he felt as if he was just a big lump of nothing.

7

Nelson's Birthday

The morning after the meeting at Jennifer Harper's home, you could already see signs that the S.O.S. committee was at work. First of all, posters appeared in the school hallways:

Save Our School!
Tell your parents to attend
the December 7 School-Board Meeting.
We need their support to
Save Our School.

When the fifth grade reported for their weekly art class, they were instructed to bring white cotton T-shirts the following week. Mrs. Boomsma, the art teacher, told them about the matching shirts with slogans that they were going to make. Julio was impressed by Jennifer's efficiency.

He knew she was behind the posters and the shirts, just as she had organized the S.O.S. meeting. And he knew that if he sat back now, it wouldn't matter. He could let Jennifer take over, and maybe she'd succeed and the Edison-Armstrong School wouldn't close after all. But Julio felt that if it turned out that Jennifer's plans didn't work out and the school did close, he would always be angry at himself. He knew he had to keep working. He just wished he could think of an original contribution for S.O.S. He wished he could think of something clever that would be a real attention getter. Something that Jennifer hadn't already thought of.

As if it wasn't bad enough that he had to figure out how to save his school, Julio was also trying hard to think of a good birthday present for his brother Nelson. In two more days, Nelson would be sixteen years old.

Last night Julio had counted his savings. He had seven dollars and forty-two cents. That included a Susan B. Anthony dollar his older brother Ramon had once given him. Julio had been saving it for good luck and in the hope that someday it would be very valuable. However, he wanted to get Nelson something good, and he decided that he would spend even this special coin in the effort.

"What are you going to give Nelson?" he had asked Ramon when Nelson wasn't listening.

"I don't know," said Ramon, shrugging. "I know he wants a car, but I can't afford that. And even if I could, he couldn't afford the gas and the insurance. Maybe I'll just promise him that he can use my car once he gets his license."

"If it starts," said Julio.

Ramon's car was so old that it probably should have been inside a museum instead of parked outside on the street. In fact, it occurred to Julio that before long, Ramon's car might be worth more sold as an antique than the Susan B. Anthony coin would be.

Mrs. Sanchez opened a box and showed Julio the sweater she had bought her son for his birthday. It was very handsome, with cable stitches and bright stripes. Still, Julio thought that Nelson should get something more exciting than clothing for his birthday.

It was after lunch that an idea for a great gift for Nelson suddenly occurred to Julio. The class was outside running around in the yard and Julio was waiting his turn to shoot some free throws when he noticed some men who were walking around the area. There were three men, and one of them had a camera. The photographer listened as the other two spoke to him. One man pointed to the front of the building, and the photographer nodded his head and walked in that direction. Julio watched as the man bent his head to focus the camera and then took a couple of pictures. It probably had something to do with the school closing, Julio thought with disgust. There were an awful lot of visitors at the school these days.

"Hey, Julio, it's your turn," shouted Lucas.

Julio hadn't even noticed that the two boys ahead of him in line had already gone. He took the ball from Lucas and stood at the foul line. He dribbled three times, as his brother had taught him, and just as the ball was about to leave his hand, an

79

idea popped into his head. A camera! That would be a neat gift to get for Nelson.

He was so delighted by this thought that he didn't even mind that he missed the basket.

"You get two more shots," said Lucas as Julio turned to walk away.

"That's okay. Someone else can go." Julio walked off. He wanted to watch the photographer and listen to what the men were saying.

"Did you go to this school?" one of the men asked the others. He had a mustache, but his head was completely bald.

"No. I lived on the other side of town," said the man with the camera. "I went to Thomas Jefferson."

"I didn't live around here either," said the second man. "Did you?"

"No," said the bald man who asked the question. "I grew up in Rawley."

"Where's that?"

"It's a very small town, north of here. About seventy miles or so. The funny thing is, my school is gone too. I was in the area a couple of years ago and drove past my old home. Then I got the idea to drive by my school, just for old times' sake. I couldn't find it. I drove around and around in circles for about half an hour. I thought I was lost or going crazy. But it turned out that they had torn down the building, and there were three new houses on the site. It made me feel—"

The bell signaling the end of recess rang and drowned out the last of the man's words. Julio wondered if the Edison-Armstrong building would be torn down if it was sold. That was even worse than just selling the building to someone for another use. Julio wanted to hear how the man felt about his school being gone, but Lucas came over and pulled him along.

"Come on," Lucas shouted at him. "We gotta go back inside."

So there were two things floating around inside Julio's head all afternoon: the words of the man whose school had disappeared and the idea of buying a camera for Nelson.

"Wake up, Julio," Mr. Flores said a couple of times. But it was hard for Julio to pay attention when his head was so filled with other things.

Julio knew his seven dollars and forty-two cents would not be enough money for a camera. But he hoped that the other members of his family would like his idea enough to chip in and pay too. When he got home, he started to explain his plan to his grandmother.

"Not now, later," she said in Spanish, putting her finger to her lips. She was engrossed in her usual soap operas. Sometimes Julio thought that the things that happened on the television screen were more real to his grandmother than her own life.

So he ate a banana and a piece of cheese that he found in the refrigerator and waited until the kissing and the crying and the yelling was over on the television.

"So what is it?" asked the old woman as she fixed herself a cup of instant coffee.

"It's about Nelson's birthday," said Julio. "I got a great idea for a present for him. A camera! Will you help me pay for it?"

"That's a good idea," said his grandmother. "Then he could take my picture." She reached for her black pocketbook, which was hanging over a chair. She opened it and took out her coin purse.

"Here," she said, and she handed Julio a five-dollar bill. "You boys are worth much more than money to me," she explained to her grandson. "I wish I was very rich and could buy you everything you ever wanted. But even if I could, that wouldn't be a good thing for you. So it's just as well I'm a poor old lady."

"Hey. You're not so old," said Julio. "A girl in my class has a great-grandfather who is eighty. That's as old as my school building."

Ramon had fewer words but more money to offer Julio. "Great!" he said. "Do you want me to buy it? There's a camera shop in the mall right near the college."

"Sure," said Julio. He handed over all his money and the money from his grandmother too. He didn't know anything about cameras, so he was relieved not to have the responsibility of actually selecting the present.

On Friday evening Julio, Nelson, Ramon, their mother, their grandmother, their great-aunt Gladys, who was their grandmother's sister, and Ramon's girlfriend, Yolanda, all sat around the table, eating the birthday dinner.

"Sixteen!" said Aunt Gladys. "I can remember when you were wearing diapers."

"Hey. Forget that. It was a long time ago," said Nelson, blushing.

"Yesterday. It seems to me it was yesterday." Aunt Gladys turned to her sister for support.

"Not yesterday," their grandmother said. "But not so very long ago."

"Now you're a man," said Aunt Gladys. "Just like Ramon."

"Sure," said Yolanda. "Next week he's going out on a date with my sister Corinne. The four of us are going out together."

Julio could see that Nelson was uncomfortable with all this talk about diapers and dates.

"When can we give Nelson his presents?" he asked.

"Yeah," said Nelson. "When do I get my presents?"

"Right now," said Mrs. Sanchez. She went to the kitchen and returned with a cake covered with a gooey chocolate frosting. "This is from Aunt Gladys. She made it special for your birthday, and how she ever got it here on the bus, I'll never know."

"About half the people on the bus wanted to

come and join us when they saw it," said Aunt Gladys, smiling proudly. "But I told them I wanted to be sure my nephew Nelson got second and third helpings. He's a growing boy."

Julio laughed. In five minutes Nelson had been a baby, a man, and a growing boy.

Ramon reached behind the living-room couch, where they had hidden the other gifts for Nelson. There was the woolen sweater in a big box, the camera in a medium-sized box, and three rolls of film from Yolanda in a small box with silver wrapping paper and a huge bow.

Julio could see that Nelson was pleased. He turned the camera over and over, admiring it.

"Take a picture of my cake," said Aunt Gladys. "That way you won't forget it."

So before anyone could have a slice of cake, Nelson had to load the camera and take a picture. Then he took another picture of all his family squeezed together on one side of the table.

"Now Ramon should take a picture of Nelson," instructed Aunt Gladys. "But first put on your new sweater."

Julio had forgotten how bossy Aunt Gladys could be at times. Still, he knew she made the very

best chocolate cake in the world. She had made one for his birthday too.

So he sat waiting patiently while Nelson put on his sweater and posed for Ramon. And as he sat, he fingered the Susan B. Anthony dollar in his pocket. Ramon had brought it home to him and told him to keep it because he'd had enough money.

"All right," said Nelson, sitting back at his place. "Now I'm going to cut the cake."

"Give Julio a big piece," said Aunt Gladys. "He's a growing boy too."

Julio smiled at his great-aunt. Too bad she wasn't on the S.O.S. committee, he thought. She probably could teach even Jennifer Harper a thing or two about how to get things done.

8

The School-Board Meeting

Several small magnets saying COME BACK TO SYCAMORE SHADE MOTEL were on the refrigerator in Julio's kitchen at home. All the guests at Sycamore Shade received a magnet with their final bill. As a motel employee for almost eight years, Mrs. Sanchez had a considerable supply of the magnets. She used them to attach notes and photographs. Now a reminder about the school-board meeting was hanging on the refrigerator door.

"So, will you come?" Julio nagged his mother. He had already been turned down by his brothers. Ramon had two college classes that met on the same evening as the school-board meeting. As for Nelson, he was taking a big math test the morning after the meeting, and he needed the time for studying.

"What difference will it make if I'm there or not?" asked Mrs. Sanchez.

Julio shrugged. "I'm not sure. But we're hoping that lots of parents show up and protest the school closing. Maybe then the people on the school board will change their plans." He was feeling discouraged. The school board had sent a typed two-sentence letter to his class:

> *The board thanks you for your interest in our current discussion about the future of Edison-Armstrong School. The matter will be debated at the next meeting, on December 7.*

"All right," said his mother. "But don't expect me to stand up and make a speech or anything like that. I'll just be another body in the audience."

"Great," said Julio, hugging his mother. "How about bringing Grandma too? She could be another body."

So that was why Mrs. Sanchez and her mother, who didn't even know enough English to follow the proceedings, were sitting in the high school auditorium at 7:30 on the evening of December 7. The hall was mobbed. Julio saw many of his classmates, accompanied by their parents. He saw Jennifer Harper rushing down the aisle to a front seat next to her mother. She was waving to all her friends as she went. Julio looked around. He was sure Mr. Flores was somewhere in the auditorium too, but he couldn't spot him in the crowd.

"It looks like they are giving away something," said Julio's grandmother in Spanish as she looked around at the huge gathering. "Maybe some coffee and cake?" she asked hopefully.

"They want to give away my school," Julio tried to explain. "But we're not going to let them."

Lucas Cott, who knew a lot of history, had told Julio that this meeting was on the anniversary of the bombing of Pearl Harbor: December 7, 1941. "That was the reason the United States entered the Second World War," Lucas said. Julio felt that he and his classmates were fighting a war too. He didn't know if they were going to be strong enough to win, but seeing so many people in the audience was certainly reassuring.

On the other hand, Julio didn't know that school-board meetings were so dull. The five board members sat at a long table up on the stage. There were microphones at each place so that everyone could hear what they had to say. It looked like one of those very serious discussion programs on television, which Julio always turned off.

First there was the reading of the minutes of the last meeting by one of the board members, Mrs. Milisock. There were lots of numbers and talk about contracts and bids. Julio's grandmother settled back in her seat and quickly fell asleep. Julio gave her a little poke when she began to snore.

After the minutes, there was old business. The members voted to build a drinking fountain in the school yard at Thomas Jefferson. They discussed the bids they had received from a furniture supplier and the permanent appointment of the acting custodian to replace the one at George Washington who had been advised by his doctor to take early retirement. It was stuffy in the auditorium, and Julio caught himself almost nodding off. In another moment his grandmother would probably have to poke him for snoring, just as he had poked her.

But finally, after the most boring forty minutes of his life, the action began. The school-board president, Mr. Schreckengost, began reading a report that he had put together. It listed the cost of maintaining the Edison-Armstrong School—things like heating, electricity, repairs, and insurance. He explained that by closing the school thousands of dollars could be saved each year.

As Mr. Schreckengost spoke, there was an undercurrent of mumbling throughout the audience. As soon as he stopped for breath, dozens of hands were raised in the audience.

"I'm not finished," Mr. Schreckengost said angrily. "Let me finish, and you'll agree with my conclusions."

"Don't jump to conclusions for us," a loud male voice called out. It was the father of one of the Edison-Armstrong students.

"When I finish, you'll have a chance to speak," said Mr. Schreckengost. "Anyone who wishes to have the floor will be asked to form a single line along the left-hand wall."

Instantly men and women were jumping out of their seats and rushing across the room. Julio grinned when he saw that the line was the length of the entire auditorium and seemed to go out into the street.

He recognized Jennifer Harper's mother at the head of the line. She apparently had come to enough board meetings in the past to know exactly where to station herself in order to be first in line.

Mr. Schreckengost cleared his throat and continued his report. He told how Edison-Armstrong was the oldest school building in the district. Therefore it needed the most repairs annually. Heating was not as efficient and lighting not as good as in the other, more modern buildings.

As he spoke, more and more people left their seats and got into the line so that they could express their opinions on all this too. At this rate, Julio thought, soon he and his mother and grandmother might be the only people left sitting in the auditorium—except for the school-board members on the stage.

Finally Mr. Schreckengost concluded his talk. "The board will now hear from those members of the audience who wish to speak," he said. "Please state your name before you begin your comments."

Jennifer's mother moved deliberately toward a microphone that had been turned on in the front of the auditorium. "Lillian Harper," she said in a loud, clear voice. "I am the mother of Jennifer, who is a sixth-grade student at Edison-Armstrong, so you might think that all of what you said does not affect my family at all. However, I am speaking tonight on behalf of all those parents whose children were scheduled to continue at Edison-Armstrong next year and even those whose children were to begin attending next year. Mr. Schreckengost, you read a lot of numbers to us. But I didn't hear a single figure for transportation. What about the cost of maintaining extra buses to drive Edison-Armstrong students to the other district schools farther away from their homes? What about the cost of hiring bus drivers? What about the insurance rates?"

Loud cheers covered up the rest of Mrs. Harper's words.

The next speaker identified himself as George Rogers, father of Traci and Erin, who attended

Thomas Jefferson. "The school my daughters go to has four hundred thirty-seven students," he said. "If only half of the Edison-Armstrong students are sent to Thomas Jefferson next year, there will be close to seven hundred children. I have nothing against any of those children, but such a huge increase in numbers from one year to the next will totally change the character of Thomas Jefferson. I think you should seriously reconsider what you want to do before you so glibly talk about closing one school building and packing the children into another."

Julio started to feel better and better. It hadn't occurred to him that parents from the other schools in the district would speak out in favor of keeping his school open. This was like watching a baseball game and his team had a lot of home-run hitters. They could win this game after all, he thought.

But then the next speaker came to the microphone. "Harold Rojahn," he identified himself. "I am an accountant, so I am especially concerned with the question of the economics of this move. There is no question that the school district can save a great deal of money, even after leasing additional buses and paying insurance costs for them. In my opinion, closing Edison-Armstrong is a good plan."

"Where do your kids go to school?" someone called out.

"My children are both in high school now," Mr. Rojahn responded. "Originally they attended George Washington. It was a fine school."

"It won't be if it gets three hundred new students overnight," called out George Rogers.

Julio looked on in amazement. The grown-ups were yelling comments out of turn and interrupting one another like little kids. Mr. Schreckengost

had to shout several times to quiet the audience and regain order.

After a while Julio lost track. There were too many parents and too many points of view. Some agreed that Edison-Armstrong should stay open. Others felt it should close. A lot of people seemed to be repeating things that had been said a few minutes before by someone else. It was no longer so exciting to hear what everyone had to say. There were home runs and foul balls on both sides, and Julio no longer felt confident of winning. In fact, by the time his mother leaned over and told him that she wanted to leave, Julio didn't have the

energy or even the interest to protest. It was after eleven at night. Although some of the people waiting for a chance to speak had given up and gone on home, there were still about twenty or so determined men and women waiting their turn.

Mr. Schreckengost and the other board members looked exhausted too. "I move that we adjourn this meeting and continue our discussion at our next scheduled meeting, in January," he said.

"I second the motion," said Mrs. Milisock.

She must have been worn out taking all those notes for the minutes, Julio thought.

"One more meeting may not be enough to solve all this," said Mrs. Sanchez as she helped her mother put on her winter coat.

"At least they should serve refreshments," complained Julio's grandmother. "There was no coffee and cake and no kissing. I like my television shows better than all this."

"Thanks for coming, *Abuela*," said Julio with a sigh. "I'm sorry you didn't get anything to eat." He leaned over and pressed his lips against her cheek. "At least you get a little kissing."

9

Nelson Sanchez, Photographer

On Saturday morning, Julio was awakened by a flashbulb going off in his face. It was Nelson taking another picture with his birthday camera. Julio was glad that Nelson liked his present so much. But it was getting to be a real pain having flashes going off when he least expected it.

"We have created a monster," Ramon had observed earlier to Julio.

In one week Nelson had managed to use all three rolls of film he received on his birthday. He had photographed his family in every imaginable pose: eating, sleeping, talking, scratching. He'd even taken a picture of Julio blowing his nose.

"Models usually get a pretty good fee for posing," Mrs. Sanchez said to Nelson.

"When I become a professional photographer, I'll have lots of money to give you," Nelson promised.

In addition to using three rolls of film this week, Nelson had also changed his life goals. He no longer wanted to become an engineer. He now wanted to work for a newspaper as a photographer. He already was making plans to take a photography course given by the art department at his high school next semester. He wanted to learn how to develop his own pictures.

As Julio ate his bowl of cornflakes, he got an idea. "I'm going to Lucas's house now to play. How about coming and taking a photo of Lucas and me?" he asked Nelson. "He's my best friend, and it would be neat to have our picture taken together."

"Sure," agreed Nelson. "I've run out of people to photograph around here. I don't have to be at work until one o'clock."

An hour later Nelson had used another full roll of film. Only three of the pictures he'd taken were of Lucas and Julio. The rest were of Lucas's four-year-old twin brothers, Marcus and Marius.

Nelson had never met the twins before, and he was fascinated. The boys were identical, and he tried posing them in mirror images of one another. Lucas and Julio looked on, amazed. Usually the twins seemed to have too much energy to keep still for very long. They were always running and jumping about. But for some reason they responded to all of Nelson's directions. When he said "hold still," they actually did.

"I haven't had any good pictures of the boys lately," Lucas's mother, Mrs. Cott, said. "I'll pay for the roll of film and the developing."

"Let's see if the pictures come out," warned Nelson. "I'm still learning a lot about it all. Some people think that all you need to do is point the camera and push the button. But good pictures need more than that."

Nelson went off to a one-hour developing shop in the neighborhood. Julio was still at Lucas's home when Nelson returned with the finished pictures. Everyone agreed that they were wonderful. His pictures really captured Marcus and Marius in a natural manner. Even though he had told them not to move, when you looked at the photo-

graphs, you thought they were about to move in the next instant. They did not look stilted or posed at all.

"There's no question you have the knack for this," said Mrs. Cott, admiring the pictures of her sons. "Can I borrow the negatives? I want to get a couple of these enlarged."

Nelson gave Julio one of the shots he had taken of him together with Lucas. After all, that was the reason he had come over here in the first place. Then he gave the remainder of the pictures and the negatives to Mrs. Cott.

She in turn reimbursed Nelson for the film and the developing costs. "I really feel I should pay you something for your work too. I'd have paid a studio photographer if I had taken the boys in to one. Only the last time we went, Marcus and Marius chased each other around the room and knocked one of his lamps onto the floor."

"It broke," Lucas explained. "And Mom had to pay for it."

"It was a very expensive and wearing experience," Mrs. Cott remembered. "Here. Take this toward your next rolls of film." She pressed a bill into Nelson's hand.

"Gosh. Thank you. I feel like a real professional, getting paid for taking pictures," said Nelson, blushing. "I'm glad you like them."

Julio was proud of his brother. And he was proud too of his role in finding this new interest for him. Walking home with Nelson a little later, Julio suddenly had an idea. Even Jennifer Harper hadn't thought of this one.

"When Mrs. Cott returns the negatives, could we make another copy of one of the pictures of the twins? Maybe blow it up bigger too."

"What are you going to do with it?" asked Nelson.

"I just thought how great one of those pictures would be in a poster," said Julio excitedly. "*Keep Edison-Armstrong open for the little kids.*" He could hardly wait to make the poster and bring it in to school.

"You sure are obsessed with keeping that school open," said Nelson. He pulled a package of gum out of his pocket and offered it to his brother.

"I know," agreed Julio, taking a stick of gum. "I'm not going to let them close it without a fight."

"One school is as good or as bad as another,"

said Nelson as he folded a piece of gum into his mouth.

"No. That's not true," argued Julio. "All schools have teachers and desks and papers and tests. But Edison-Armstrong has continuity and history as well. I care about it, and that's why I don't want it to be shut down."

He watched as Nelson threw the wrapper from his gum onto the street. "See, there are two kinds of people. Those who just think of the moment and who throw their gum wrappers and empty cigarette packs and other garbage out on the street. And then there's people like me." He took his gum wrapper and stuffed it into his jacket pocket. "If everyone throws trash in the street, soon we won't be able to walk, because there will be too much garbage in the way. If we shut down all the old buildings, we'll lose all sense of history."

"Don't exaggerate," said Nelson. "And don't look at me like I'm a criminal just because I threw a little piece of paper on the ground. Besides, I don't smoke. So I don't throw cigarette packs on the street."

"It all adds up. Even little pieces," said Julio.

Nelson shrugged. But he bent down and retrieved the gum wrapper from the ground. He put it in his pocket.

"Okay, okay. I got the point," he said, and the two brothers continued walking home together.

10

The Big Assembly

Every year for as far back as anyone could remember, there was a huge holiday music program given by the students of Edison-Armstrong. It was presented twice. There was an evening program at seven-thirty for parents who would not be able to attend during the daytime. The second performance was given the next day. Even before Thanksgiving, music classes were busy learning Christmas carols and other holiday songs. Certain songs were traditionally reserved for each grade. There were few surprises at the program, but everyone always enjoyed it anyway. At eighteen,

Julio's brother Ramon still remembered all the words to the songs he had sung when he was a little kid at Edison-Armstrong.

This year, at the urging of Jennifer Harper and the other S.O.S. members, Mr. Herbertson agreed to the unthinkable. The theme of the holiday program would be Edison-Armstrong's history. As a compromise, they would still sing a few seasonal songs. After all, the principal pointed out, the holiday assembly with singing was part of the school's history. But by and large this was an original program with new songs whose words were written by the students, even if the melodies seemed very familiar.

Anne Crosby had brought in the words to the song she had written:

> *Edison-Armstrong,*
> *We are strong,*
> *So don't get me wrong*
> *When I sing this song.*
> *It's Edison-Armstrong—*
> *We're the best all along.*
>
> *We're the very best.*
> *Put us to any test—*

Then you'll see the rest.
Haven't you ever guessed
It's Edison-Armstrong
All along?

Mr. Flores said he didn't think the words would work with any of the traditional holiday music. But he would figure out a simple melody so that everyone in the class could sing together.

Cricket, Zoe, Arthur, and Franklin had done serious research in the library. They were going to tell the audience what was happening in the world eighty years ago, when their school building was being constructed.

Julio was going to present material about the man their school was named after. He had gone to the library and read up on the famous inventor. He was sorry to discover that Thomas Edison lived from 1847 to 1931. There was no way he could have been a student at their school. In fact, he had hardly gone to any school at all. His mother had been his teacher, and she'd taught him at home. Julio didn't think he should mention that in his report.

Julio already knew that Edison was famous for his invention of the electric light, but he hadn't realized that Edison also worked on perfecting the typewriter, the phonograph, the telephone, and the electric generator. He even helped invent the camera and moving pictures. He had been born in Ohio and moved when he was a kid to Michigan. But for most of his adult life he lived in New Jersey, in Menlo Park and then in West Orange. That wasn't too far away from the town where Julio lived. No wonder the school had picked the name of this famous inventor for the building.

Jennifer Harper stopped Julio in the school yard the next morning to tell him that she was sending invitations to all the board members to attend the holiday assembly. "The newspaper is going to cover it, and my mother has been on the phone with the local television station too," she said.

Julio nodded his head. He knew he should be more appreciative of all Jennifer and her mother were doing. But he resented that she had taken over and made this her own personal mission. It was as if she was the only one who cared about the future of the school.

"I've got a great idea for a poster," Julio said. He explained to Jennifer about the photograph his brother had taken of Lucas's twin brothers.

Jennifer shrugged. "Posters are okay," she said, "but I don't think they make any difference in the long run. After all, who sees them? Just us. That's why it's important to get the newspaper and the television coverage of the assembly."

Julio felt more annoyed with Jennifer than ever. It seemed that no matter what he suggested, it wasn't good enough for her. "How about inviting everyone in town who is eighty or over to come to the assembly too?" he asked.

"What good will that do?" responded Jennifer.

"Well. The school is eighty years old. Some of them may have lived here and will remember when the place was built," said Julio.

"I don't think that will influence the school board one way or the other," said Jennifer. "Forget it."

But Julio didn't forget it, and he asked Mr. Flores what he thought.

"That's a great idea," the teacher agreed. "How can we notify those senior citizens about our assembly?"

"I'll ask my father if they can put something in the newspaper," offered Zoe.

"Great!" said Julio, socking his right fist into his left hand. Despite Jennifer and her bossy ways, he liked the way the assembly was shaping up. He decided he was going to go ahead and make his poster too. He wasn't going to let Jennifer discourage him.

On the evening of the assembly, the school building was packed. The teachers' parking lot was so full that cars lined the streets for blocks around.

There was no auditorium in the Edison-Armstrong School, so the program was being held in the gym. Folding chairs had been set up for the parents, and students sat in class groups on the floor. All the students, from kindergarten through sixth grade, were wearing their newly designed T-shirts. The six hundred yellow shirts were a very striking sight. Just as Jennifer planned, every shirt said on the front:

Keep the lights on at
Edison-Armstrong School

On the back of every shirt was picture of a light bulb. It might be Jennifer's message, thought Julio. But he felt very proud that he had convinced Jennifer and the other S.O.S. committee members that the shirts should be yellow, to represent light.

Julio waved to his mother and grandmother. He had promised his grandmother that this was an evening she would enjoy much better than the school-board meeting. He had to admit to her, however, that there wouldn't be any coffee and cake this time either.

He looked around to see if he could spot the members of the school board in the audience. They had all been invited. He hoped they would notice the poster he had made and taped right in the entrance hallway of the school:

Keep our school open for the little kids.
They deserve the best too.

Underneath the words was an enlargement of one of the great pictures Nelson had taken of Marcus and Marius. Julio had checked with Mrs. Cott. She had no objection to her sons being on the poster. The twins looked so angelic that you would never guess what demons they could also be.

Cricket gave Julio a poke. "Look over there," she hissed. "I see Mrs. Milisock and Mr. Schreckengost." That meant two of the five board members had come to the assembly. Perhaps the others would come later, or tomorrow.

Julio saw a man with a video camera taking pictures. He didn't know if the man was from the local television station or if he was a parent. Maybe he was both, Julio thought hopefully. Then he would want to stay for the full assembly and would fight to get more of the film on the news.

The little kindergarten children sang "Jingle Bells." They did it every year, and even on a night when traditions were being broken, that one remained. They waved ribbons with bells attached to them as they sang. Julio remembered when he was five years old and did the same thing. He had thought it was such a big deal to come back to school at night to sing with his classmates. How he had loved waving those bells!

The other grades, however, had new words to sing to the holiday tunes. So though the audience was listening to the melodies of "Deck the Halls," "God Rest Ye, Merry Gentlemen," and "Dreidel, Dreidel, Dreidel," each song had been transformed to praise their school or lament its closing.

When Mr. Flores's class had its turn, everyone sang the song that Anne Crosby had written, and their teacher accompanied them on his guitar. Then, while the others sat down, Cricket, Zoe, Arthur, and Franklin remained standing and recited bits of historic information about life in America eighty years ago. Cricket and Zoe even wore old-fashioned hats like women wore in those days. Probably Henrietta Armstrong, the first principal, had come to school wearing a funny-looking hat like that too.

Then it was Julio's turn. Being class president had shown him he had abilities that he hadn't known he possessed. But standing in front of a huge audience was not one of them. He walked nervously to the front of the gym and took the portable microphone that was handed to him by Zoe. He remembered how in the past, he and Lucas had loved to grab the school mike when they got a chance and listen to their voices magnified. Now he was scared. He wished he was sitting on the floor with the rest of the kids in his class.

He took a deep breath and nodded his head. This was his special signal to Mr. Flores. Suddenly all the lights went out, and the gymnasium was in total darkness. Julio counted to ten as he listened to the surprised voices from the audience. They didn't know this was part of his act.

Then the lights were on again as suddenly as they had been turned off. "If it wasn't for Thomas Edison, we would all be sitting in the dark. Or at least, almost dark. We wouldn't have electric lights, and we would have to use candles or oil lamps," said Julio into the microphone. He could hear himself and was impressed by his own serious tone.

He repeated the important facts he had memorized about the inventor. Then he said, "To the students in this school, the name Thomas Edison has taken on another meaning. Together with Henrietta Armstrong, the school's first principal, it has come to stand for a place where education is important, where teachers care. It's a place where even some of your parents went to school. My older brothers Ramon and Nelson attended this school. My friend Lucas's little brothers Marcus and Marius were going to begin kindergarten here next September. Now the school is probably going to be closed. I hope it will stay open for them and that someday, when I'm a father, my children can go to this school too."

That was it. He was finished, and he hadn't

even messed up a single word. With great relief Julio sat down. He hardly noticed that he was getting a lot of applause. Lucas gave him a thump on the back.

"Wait till Marcus and Marius hear you tomorrow. They'll be all excited to hear their names in your speech."

Julio had totally forgotten he would have to repeat everything the next day. But now that he'd done it once, he supposed it wouldn't be so terrible the second time.

The sixth grade sang a couple of songs, and then Jennifer Harper asked all the students to stand. Six hundred boys and girls wearing bright yellow T-shirts scrambled to their feet and turned to face the adults sitting in the rear of the gym.

"One, two, three," Jennifer counted dramatically into the microphone. "What do you want to tell me?" she asked.

In unison, the students all chanted, "Keep the lights on at Edison-Armstrong School!"

Then every one of the students turned around and faced in the opposite direction, so that six hundred light bulbs were facing the audience.

There was no need for the students to shout.

The school spirit and the message had been evident all evening long.

One message, however, was strangely missing. As he walked out of the school building with his mother and grandmother on the way home, Julio walked over to the area where his poster was hanging. He wanted to admire it once more, and he wanted to see if anyone else was looking at it too. No one was, because the poster was no longer there. During the assembly, someone had apparently removed the poster from the wall. Who would do a thing like that? Julio wondered angrily. His mood, which had been great all evening, suddenly changed. He wondered if the missing poster could be a bad omen. Perhaps a year from now the students and teachers would be missing from this building too.

11

Repeat Performance

The repeat performance of the holiday assembly always had a different atmosphere from the first one. Partly this was because coming to the school building and giving a program at night was so out of the ordinary. Schools ceased to exist for the students after the three o'clock bell, when everyone went home. And yet there it had been, looking the same as ever and waiting for the students to return, even though the hands of the clock pointed to an hour when the boys and girls were never there.

The second performance took place in daylight. It seemed more ordinary. And yet making up for the early hour was the knowledge that after the show, students would be returning to their classrooms not for arithmetic or spelling or social studies but for a holiday party. For the second performance was given on the last morning of school before winter vacation.

When the students filed into the gym for their assembly, they had a different audience from the one that they had the night before. There were many mothers with young children. Julio saw Marcus and Marius even before they spotted him. He was still upset that his poster with their picture had disappeared. Where it had gone was a real mystery to him. None of the other posters were missing.

"Look, look!" squealed Cricket.

Julio turned to where she was pointing. He saw a section of seats that was filled by elderly men and women.

"Those must be the people who saw the notice in the newspaper. They're the ones who are eighty years old or even older and remember when our school was new," said Zoe. "My father promised me that the little piece he wrote would have results. And it did."

The assembly began. The kindergarten children rang their bells and sang just as they had the evening before. Grade by grade the program continued.

When it was Julio's turn to speak, he was sorry that turning off the lights was not as effective as it had been last night. He hadn't taken into account that there would be so much daylight at ten o'clock in the morning.

When Julio reached the mention of Marcus and Marius's names, there was no problem. Lucas had warned his mother, and she had warned the boys.

The sixth grade sang "I'm Dreaming of Edison-Armstrong" to the tune of "White Christmas," just as they had done the evening before. The song concluded with the lines "May you study here as your right, and may Edison-Armstrong win this fight."

Then Jennifer Harper called out as she had the night before, and the students gave their cheer. Mr. Herbertson, wearing a bright yellow T-shirt of his own, took center stage. "We have some special visitors with us this morning," he said to the students. "And I'd like to point them out to you.

There are seventeen people in our audience who watched this building being constructed. Mr. Edwards, who is eighty-seven years old, has agreed to speak to us. I hope you'll all give him your closest attention."

Julio watched as a white-haired man with a cane made his way toward the front of the gym. Mr. Herbertson handed the microphone to Mr. Edwards.

"Hello," said the old man in a raspy voice. "Would you believe that this is the first time I ever got inside this building?" Mr. Edwards paused and looked around at the students. Then he continued. "They started working on it when I was a kid, and I used to come every day and watch the steam shovel dig the hole that became the school's basement. I was fascinated. After all, we didn't have television at that time. Watching this school get built was like a wonderful movie or TV show for me. And it didn't cost me a penny to watch."

Julio listened thoughtfully to all Mr. Edwards had to say. He wondered what it felt like to be so old. And he wondered if his school would be here for him to visit when he was eighty-seven.

"Elementary school went up to eighth grade

in those days," the old man explained. "So I was sure that I would get inside this brand-new building when it was finished. I couldn't wait. But then my family moved away to another town. I was sorry not to come here, but you know, it influenced my life anyhow. I got so interested in construction from the days of watching this building go up that I became a contractor. And I moved back here. My company built a lot of houses in this town. You can ask your parents when you go home today. If they say that your house was made by Edwards and Edwards, you can tell them that you met the first Edwards."

There was a lot of applause when Mr. Edwards finished speaking.

"I hope you'll come back and talk to our students another time about life eighty years ago," said Mr. Herbertson. "I think they could learn a lot from you."

"I'd be glad to," said the old man.

"Good," said Mr. Herbertson. He handed Mr. Edwards a yellow T-shirt. It said:

Keep the lights on at
Edison-Armstrong School

"This will make sure you don't forget," the principal said.

"Wow!" said Lucas as the students walked back to their classrooms. "Eighty-seven. Wouldn't it be neat if we could come back here and talk to the little kids when we're eighty-seven years old?"

"There probably won't be a school here by then. There probably won't be a school here by the time we're twelve," grumbled Cricket.

"Don't be so sure," said Zoe. "My father said that there's a lot of strong feelings in town about saving Edison-Armstrong. He was very impressed with the school spirit at our assembly last night."

That was a good note on which to begin a holiday party. The students had brought in bags of potato chips and cookies, as well as bottles of soda and fruit juice. They had also each brought a small gift-wrapped package for a grab bag. There had been a lot of discussion about whether there should be separate grab bags for girls and boys. "I don't want to pull out a bunch of barrettes," Lucas had said when they were planning the party.

"There are lots of presents that are good for both boys and girls," Anne pointed out.

"You could always trade with someone if you don't like your gift," suggested Arthur.

Julio had bought a package of colored markers as his contribution. It had been on sale and cost exactly one dollar, which was the amount the class had agreed each person should spend. When it was his turn, he pulled out a giant chocolate bar. It was a good present because he could share it with his whole family.

The students were dismissed at noon, so there was no lunch served at school that day. Even if lunch had been served, no one would have had any appetite to eat it.

Mr. Flores handed each student a small holiday gift as they were leaving. "Don't open these before you get home," he warned. "If you do, I won't give you anything next year."

"You won't give us anything next year anyhow," said Franklin. "You won't be our teacher then."

"You'll have to wait and see," said Mr. Flores.

The packages were all the same size, small and light. They didn't rattle, and it was hard to guess from squeezing it what could be inside. It was still two days until Christmas, and Julio thought he should wait. However, halfway home Julio could not resist the urge. He ripped the paper off Mr. Flores's present. It was a mechanical pencil, the kind that you had to fill with thin sticks of lead. He'd always wanted one. They came in many different colors. His was blue.

If he didn't tell Mr. Flores that he'd opened it before he got home, maybe next year he'd get another gift from his teacher after all. He wondered where he'd be going to school next year, and he wondered if Mr. Flores would be teaching in the same building.

It was a good thing that his mother called to him to set the table for supper. Julio was beginning to feel sad from all his thoughts. He grabbed his large bar of chocolate from his backpack and took it into the kitchen.

"Look, Ma," he said, showing it to his mother. "This is for us to have for dessert tonight."

"How lovely," said Mrs. Sanchez. "My sweet tooth can always use a piece of chocolate." Even though her hands were wet from rinsing lettuce leaves, she gave Julio a hug.

"I know a secret," she said.

"What is it?" asked Julio.

"I can't tell you. Then it won't be a secret," teased Mrs. Sanchez. "You'll just have to wait."

12

Front Page News

The holiday season was filled with so many surprises that Julio forgot what his mother had said. Maybe she had been referring to his new Rollerblade skates. Maybe she meant the new jacket that he also got for Christmas. Maybe she'd been thinking about the overnight visit from his cousin Luis or that Luis's mother was expecting a new baby.

So with many surprises and presents and good times, the winter vacation quickly passed, and Julio tried not to think about the next school-board meeting—the one that was scheduled right after the New Year.

"I have had enough going to school meetings," Julio's grandmother said. "I went to two already. This time I'm staying home."

"Only one was a meeting," Julio protested. "The other was the school assembly. You liked that."

"That's right," agreed his grandmother. "Now I stop while I'm ahead. No more meetings for me."

"But you're coming, aren't you?" Julio begged his mother.

Mrs. Sanchez sighed. "I am so tired when I come home from work. But I'll come."

The high school was at least as crowded for the January 5 meeting as it had been a month earlier. Just as Lucas had noticed that December 7 was the anniversary of Pearl Harbor, Julio was aware that this was the eve of Epiphany. Epiphany was a Christian holiday that his mother and grandmother had celebrated when they lived in Puerto Rico. Even now, although they didn't have a big party the way they had in the past, his mother always prepared a special meal. Julio hoped that tomorrow when he was eating the food he would also be celebrating that Edison-Armstrong was to remain open.

Mr. Schreckengost called the meeting to order. Then Mrs. Milisock read the minutes of the last meeting. Julio had worried that they would have to listen to everyone's comments all over again. However, Mrs. Milisock merely read a list of the names of parents who had identified themselves and spoken at the December meeting. She didn't mention the people who called out or what their comments had been.

Julio looked up and saw that a long line had formed against the left-hand wall of the auditorium. These were the parents who wanted a turn to speak tonight. However, before any of them had a chance to get to the microphone, Mr. Schreckengost made an announcement. He cleared his throat and spoke in a voice weighty with importance. "As a result of a reevaluation of our financial study, last month's meeting, the outpouring of mail that the board has received, public opinion, and, last but not least, the moving holiday program put on by the students of Edison-Armstrong, the board has made the decision to table, indefinitely, the proposal to close the Edison-Armstrong School. It is possible that in the future we will have to close one of the schools in the district. But it seems unlikely that it will ever be Edison-Armstrong, a school with a rich tradition and history and an amazing amount of school spirit."

Mr. Schreckengost had more to say, but Julio couldn't hear it. The whole auditorium was cheering and shouting. People were standing in the aisles and hugging one another. Men were thumping each other on the back. It was a never-to-be-forgotten moment!

When the audience had finally calmed down and it was once again quiet in the auditorium, Jennifer Harper's mother waved her hand to get Mr. Schreckengost's attention. He called on her.

"Mr. Chairman," she said. "I would like you to write into the minutes that much of the credit for the movement to keep the Edison-Armstrong School open should go to one person. Without the initiative of this young student, who rallied all the students at Edison-Armstrong, it is quite possible that this evening we would be present at a gathering of a very different tone."

Julio blushed with pleasure. He hadn't known that Jennifer's mother was going to say that about him.

"Please note that Jennifer Harper, a sixth-grade student, single-handedly organized her schoolmates, for the sole purpose of keeping her school open for future generations of youngsters."

Julio sat stunned. He could not believe that Jennifer's mother had said that about her daughter and not him. And what did she mean, single-handedly? Not only had she ignored the work of Julio, but she forgot about the whole S.O.S. committee. Lots of students had worked together.

The audience broke into applause.

"Is Jennifer Harper here tonight?" asked Mr. Schreckengost.

Jennifer stood. Her hair was combed back, and she was wearing a dress. She looked like a girl who had known she was going to take the stage this evening.

"Jennifer, please come up here for a moment," said Mr. Schreckengost.

Jennifer walked to the front of the auditorium.

"Big cheese," Julio mumbled under his breath. "Who told her that the students ought to get

involved anyway?" He got even more annoyed when he saw a photographer taking pictures of Jennifer shaking hands with Mr. Schreckengost. It would probably be on the front page of tomorrow's newspaper, he thought with disgust.

There was indeed a picture of Jennifer Harper in the newspaper on January 6. But it was in the back. On the front page, next to an article about the school board's decision and the headline EDISON-ARMSTRONG TO REMAIN OPEN FOR THE NEXT GENERATION, was a photograph of Marcus and Marius. In small letters underneath the picture, credit was given to the photographer, Nelson Sanchez.

"I knew all about it," said Julio's mother, beaming as the family sat around the table eating breakfast. "The editor phoned here just before Christmas."

"So that's where my poster disappeared to," said Julio. He had forgotten about the missing poster.

"The editor called to ask Nelson's Social Security number. They are going to pay him twenty-five dollars for permitting them to use the picture."

"Permitting? I didn't even know," said Nelson. But he wasn't complaining. It was a big honor for him to have a photograph he had taken on the front page of the newspaper. "Twenty-five dollars will buy a lot of rolls of film," he added.

At school Mr. Flores took Julio aside. "I saw in the newspaper that Jennifer Harper got all the credit for student activities," he said.

"Yeah," said Julio. Why did his teacher have to rub it in?

"Just remember," said Mr. Flores. "Your goal was achieved. A year from now, it won't matter which student was praised for the work. What will matter is that this school will still be open. That's what you really wanted, wasn't it?"

"Yes," said Julio, nodding his head.

"I personally am very proud of what you did. You showed wonderful leadership ability and school spirit. You helped rally everyone in this class. No class president could have done a better job than that."

Julio blushed at his teacher's praise.

"I saw the picture your brother took on the front page too," said Mr. Flores. "Your mother should be very proud of you both."

"She's proud of my brother Ramon too," bragged Julio. "He got A's in both of the college courses he took."

"Great!" said Mr. Flores. "She's a lucky woman having three such sons. And I'm lucky to have you in my class."

As Julio walked home at the end of the day, Mr. Flores's words were still echoing in his head. It wasn't every day that he heard so many nice things about himself. There was just one thing that was still troubling him, however. The good news about Edison-Armstrong could well be somebody else's bad news. Mr. Schreckengost said that it was possible that someday one of the other schools would have to close. Julio hoped that there would be a student at George Washington or Thomas Jefferson who would have enough school spirit to rally the students.

"Hold still," a voice commanded Julio.

It was Nelson, camera in hand, just getting off the bus from the high school. "I want to take your picture."

"You've taken a hundred of me already," Julio shouted. "Find another subject." And he began running home from school, with Nelson, who had just begun his career as a news photographer, laughing and chasing after him.

It was a good thing that Nelson caught up with his younger brother, because at the apartment door Julio discovered that he didn't have his key in his pocket.